This LADYBIRD TALE
belongs to

....

Pinocchio

Retold by Audrey Daly
with illustrations by Victoria Assanelli

LADYBIRD TALES

THIS IS THE STRANGE story of a piece of wood – that became a puppet – that became a real live boy!

It all started when Antonio the carpenter took a piece of wood from the pile in the corner of his workshop. It was quite an ordinary piece of wood – nothing much to look at. Then, as Antonio raised his sharp axe to take off the bark, a little voice said, "Please don't hit me too hard!"

Antonio was afraid. He looked all round his workshop, then down at the piece of wood. "No, no," he thought. "I'm dreaming." And lifting his axe once more, he hit the piece of wood very hard.

"Oh, you've hurt me!" cried the same little voice.

Now Antonio was really frightened, but just at that moment his friend Geppetto came to the door. Geppetto had no children of his own, and he wanted a piece of wood to make into a puppet that could dance and jump and move just like a real boy.

Thankfully Antonio gave him the piece of wood that had given him such a fright. Geppetto went off with it happily and began to make his new puppet right away. "I shall call him Pinocchio," he thought as he worked. "That's a good name."

As soon as he made the puppet's face, its eyes moved and its mouth laughed. Then, as Geppetto finished the feet, Pinocchio kicked him on the nose.

Geppetto was pleased with his new puppet, in spite of its tricks. He showed Pinocchio how to walk, one foot in front of the other.

Instantly the puppet ran into the street! Geppetto ran after him, but he was too slow.

Pinocchio ran along the street and straight into the arms of a policeman! The policeman gave him back to Geppetto, but the other people in the street felt sorry for Pinocchio. They said that Geppetto was a bully.
The policeman listened to them, and he took Geppetto to prison.

While poor Geppetto was being taken to prison for something he hadn't done, Pinocchio ran home. He lay down in the house, very pleased with himself.

Then he heard a little voice not far away. Pinocchio was frightened. He turned and saw a big cricket walking slowly up the wall.

"I'm the talking cricket," it said. "There's something I must tell you."

"Chirp away, Cricket," said Pinocchio. "It makes no difference to me what you say. I'm running away from here tomorrow. If I don't, I shall have to go to school like other boys. I don't want to learn anything. I don't want to work. All I want to do is have a good time."

The cricket sighed. "I'm really sorry for you, Pinocchio. You'll end up in prison."

This made Pinocchio so cross that he threw a hammer at the cricket – and the cricket vanished.

Now Pinocchio was hungry, for he had eaten nothing all day. The only food in the house was an egg, but when Pinocchio tried to cook it, a chicken hatched out and flew away.

Pinocchio set out into the wet stormy night to find food, but no one would give him any.

At last he went home, put his feet by the fire to dry them and fell sound asleep.

Of course Pinocchio's feet were made of wood, so bit by bit they burnt away as he slept. Suddenly, there was a knock at the door. It was Geppetto!

The puppet tried to run to open the door – and fell on the floor.

"I can't open it," he shouted. "My feet have gone."

Geppetto was very cross as he climbed through the window. He thought Pinocchio was playing another of his tricks. Then he saw that the puppet really had no feet, and he was sorry.

Pinocchio was so hungry
that Geppetto gave him his
own breakfast of three pears.
As soon as he had eaten them
however, the puppet began to
ask for new feet.

But Geppetto wanted to teach
him a lesson, so he left him
to cry for a long time.

At last Pinocchio promised to
be good and go to school, and
Geppetto made him two beautiful
new feet. He even made him
some clothes.

All Pinocchio needed now was
a spelling book, but there was
no money to buy one.

Geppetto was sad because he couldn't help. Then he had an idea. He ran out of the house into the snow, putting on his old coat as he went.

Soon he came back – with a spelling book, but without his coat. He had sold his coat to buy the book for his puppet son!

As soon as the snow stopped, Pinocchio set out for school. As he went, he told himself that one day he would earn lots of money to buy Geppetto a really beautiful coat to repay him.

Suddenly there was the sound
of music in the distance. What
could it be? Pinocchio stood
still, listening. Then he made
up his mind. He could always
go to school tomorrow instead.
He ran towards the sound of
the music.

The music came from the
Great Puppet Theatre! But
Pinocchio had no money to go in.
He thought for a moment, then
he sold his spelling book for two
pence. Poor Geppetto, shivering
at home in the cold because he
bought Pinocchio a spelling book!

But Pinocchio had forgotten all
about Geppetto.

As he went into the theatre he felt really at home. The puppets welcomed him warmly and the play stopped as they said hello.

The puppets had a master called Fire-eater. He was very fierce, with a long black beard. He saw that the play had stopped because of Pinocchio, and he was angry.

At first he was going to throw Pinocchio on the fire. Then he decided to forgive him and put Harlequin on the fire instead.

But brave Pinocchio said he would die. At last Fire-eater forgave them both.

The puppets were so happy that they clapped and danced all night.

Next day, Fire-eater gave Pinocchio five gold coins to take to his father, Geppetto, and sent him home very pleased with himself.

Pinocchio was determined to be good this time, but he was soon in trouble again.

He met a wicked fox who pretended to be lame, and a cat who pretended to be blind. They tried to steal his money, but he ran away from them.

The villains chased after Pinocchio and caught him! They were so cross that they tied Pinocchio to an oak tree and left him all alone.

A little while later, a girl with blue hair saw him from her house nearby. She was really a fairy in disguise, and she sent her servants to help the puppet.

The fairy gave Pinocchio some medicine to make him well, then she asked him his story. Pinocchio told the truth to start with.

Then when he came to the part about the gold pieces, he told a lie. He said he had lost them, but they were in his pocket!

As soon as he told this lie, Pinocchio's nose grew two inches longer! Then he told another lie – and his nose grew longer still, and went on growing.

The puppet's nose grew so long because of his lies that he couldn't get out of the door.

The fairy laughed and laughed at Pinocchio as she watched, and he began to cry. He cried and cried for a long time before the fairy forgave him for telling lies. Then, at last, she called in some woodpeckers to help him. They pecked and pecked at his nose until it was the right length again, and Pinocchio was happy once more.

The fairy was fond of Pinocchio, even though he was so naughty. She wanted him to stay with her. Pinocchio said he was going home to his father Geppetto, but the fairy said that Geppetto was coming to stay, too!

Pinocchio was so pleased and excited when he heard this that he set out to meet Geppetto. He hadn't seen him for a long time.

Pinocchio was looking forward to seeing Geppetto again, but it was not to be. The wicked fox and cat turned up once more, and stole his gold pieces. When Pinocchio told a policeman about it, *he* was put in prison – for four whole months. He couldn't understand this at all.

When he came out of prison,
the puppet went back to find the
fairy. When he came to the right
place, the house was nowhere to
be seen!

As Pinocchio stood there crying
because his fairy had gone,
a pigeon flew down. It told him
that Geppetto was so unhappy
that he had gone to sea in a boat
to look for Pinocchio. This made
the puppet cry even more because
he missed Geppetto, too.

The pigeon was sorry for him.
It took him on its back to
the sea to find Geppetto.
Once more Pinocchio was
unlucky – a dolphin told him
that Geppetto had been swallowed
by a terrible shark!

Now Pinocchio found himself
on an island where everyone
worked so hard that they were
called Busy Bees. Pinocchio was
hungry – but he wasn't going to
work for his food.

Soon he was so hungry that he
had to work. He helped a woman
to carry some water. When she
gave him some food, he saw she
was his own fairy! He had found
her again.

Pinocchio told the fairy he was tired of being a puppet. He wanted to become a real live boy.

She said he could only become a real boy if he was good and obedient. He must never tell lies, and he must go to school.
So Pinocchio went to school.
He worked so hard that he became top of his class, and the fairy was pleased. She promised that soon he would become a real boy.

But there were bad boys in the class. They led him astray and Pinocchio ran away again!

This time he went to Toyland
with some other naughty boys.
They were all changed into
donkeys – ears, tails and all!

Pinocchio became a donkey in
a circus. One day he fell and hurt
his leg as he was jumping through
the hoop. This made him lame,
so he was sold for his skin to be
made into a drum.

His new master threw him into
the sea to drown – and he became
a puppet again.

Pinocchio's adventures still weren't over. As he lay at the bottom of the sea, he was swallowed by a shark. It was the same terrible shark that had swallowed his father Geppetto – and Geppetto was still alive! Pinocchio made a plan, and led him out through the shark's mouth to safety.

Now Pinocchio worked so hard to look after his poor father that the fairy forgave him for the third and final time, and gave him his wish.

So – at last – he became a real live boy.

A History of
Pinocchio

The story of *Pinocchio*, a puppet
who wants to be a real boy, is perhaps
the most popular children's story ever
to have come out of Italy. It was written
by a journalist called Carlo Collodi.

The story was originally written
as a serial for a children's magazine
and the first instalment was published
in July 1881. In 1883 the complete story
was published in book form and it
quickly became a bestseller.

When M. A. Murray first translated
Pinocchio into English in 1892,
its popularity spread to Britain
and America.

Undoubtedly the best-known version
of the story today is the one dramatized
in the 1940 Disney animated film.

Ladybird's 1979 retelling, written
by Audrey Daly, captures all the magic
and adventure of the original tale.

Collect more fantastic

LADYBIRD 🐞 TALES

Little Red Riding Hood

9781409311126

Goldilocks and the Three Bears

9781409311119

Cinderella

9781409311072

Jack and the Beanstalk

9781409311102

The Gingerbread Man

9781409311096

The Three Little Pigs

9781409311089

The Three Billy Goats Gruff

9781409311065

Hansel and Gretel

9781409311133

Puss in Boots

9781409311225

Rapunzel

9781409311195

Rumpelstiltskin

9781409311164

The Elves and the Shoemaker

9781409311188

Snow White and the Seven Dwarfs

9781409311171

The Enormous Turnip

9781409311218

The Magic Porridge Pot

9781409311201

Sleeping Beauty

9781409311157

The Princess
and the Frog

9780718192556

Dick
Whittington

9780718192532

The
Big Pancake

9780718192549

Beauty
and the Beast

9780718192587

The Little
Red Hen

9780718192525

The Ugly
Duckling

9780718193133

The Princess
and the Pea

9780718192570

Chicken
Licken

9780718192563

The Emperor's
New Clothes

9780723271048

The Little
Mermaid

9780723271055

Pinocchio

9780723271062

Aladdin

9780723271079

Endpapers taken from series 606d,
first published in 1964

A catalogue record for this book is available from the British Library

Published by Ladybird Books Ltd
80 Strand London WC2R 0RL
A Penguin Company

001

© Ladybird Books Ltd MMXIV

LADYBIRD and the device of a Ladybird are trademarks of Ladybird Books Ltd

ISBN: 978-0-72327-106-2

Printed in China